Fancy NANCY

Splendiferous Christmas

Joyeux Noël, everybody!

That's French for Merry Christmas.

Written by
Jane O'Connor

Illustrated by
Robin Preiss Glasser

HARPER
An Imprint of HarperCollins Publishers

For my splendiferous sister, Jill, and all the wonderful
Christmases we shared growing up—J.O'C.

For my sister Erica, my confidante and touchstone—R.P.G.

Fancy Nancy: Splendiferous Christmas
Text copyright © 2009 by Jane O'Connor
Illustrations copyright © 2009 by Robin Preiss Glasser
Printed in the U.S.A. All rights reserved. No part of this book may be used or reproduced in any manner whatsoever without
written permission except in the case of brief quotations embodied in critical articles and reviews. For information address
HarperCollins Children's Books, a division of HarperCollins Publishers, 10 East 53rd Street, New York, NY 10022.
www.harpercollinschildrens.com
Library of Congress Cataloging-in-Publication Data
O'Connor, Jane.
      Fancy Nancy: splendiferous Christmas / written by Jane O'Connor ; illustrated by Robin Preiss Glasser. — 1st ed.
            p.   cm. — (Fancy Nancy)
      Summary: Nancy is devastated, which is even worse than heartbroken, when her fancy Christmas tree topper breaks,
threatening to ruin Christmas.
      ISBN 978-0-06-123590-0 (trade bdg.) — ISBN 978-0-06-123591-7 (lib. bdg.)
      [1. Christmas tree ornaments—Fiction.   2. Christmas—Fiction.   3. Family life—Fiction.
4. Vocabulary—Fiction.]   I. Preiss-Glasser, Robin, ill.   II. Title.
PZ7.O222Fhs 2008   2008045063
[E]—dc22   CIP
                                                                    AC

Typography by Jeanne L. Hogle
09 10 11 12 13   CG/WORZ   10 9 8 7 6 5 4 3 2 1
❖
First Edition

Our house never looks fancy, except...

Ta-da!—
at Christmastime.

I love Christmas so much. It is important
to find a tree with a wonderful aroma.
(That's a fancy word for smell.)

I think bigger is always better.

But my dad says we must compromise.

That means we end up with the tree my mom wants.

On Christmas Eve, we get out the
ornaments. Some were Grandpa's
when he was a little boy.

"These are heirlooms," my mom says.
"That's fancy for things that are old and valuable."

Here is our tree topper. Isn't it just gorgeous?
I bought it last summer with all my birthday money.
(It is never too early to prepare for Christmas.)

It spins! It flashes!
It changes colors!

Hours of delight for the whole family!

We always wait for Grandpa to decorate the tree.
He'll be here very soon.

While we wait, we bake Christmas cookies.

My sister helps with the sprinkles.

Mmm, delectable!
(That's fancy for yummy!)

Guess which one I decorated.

I finish wrapping all the presents.

This quilt is for Marabelle. Put lace on anything and—voilà!—it's fancy.

I also made a tiny Christmas card for her.

Next we go caroling, which is fancy for singing Christmas songs.

"Deck the halls!"

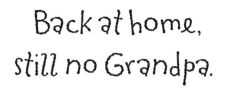

Back at home,
still no Grandpa.

So we plead with our parents.
(Pleading is like begging, only fancier.)

"Please, please,
pretty please, can we
just put up the tree
topper now?"

Ooh la la! Everything it says on the box is true! It spins. It flashes on and off and changes color.

My dad says that Grandpa called.
He'll be here any minute.

We wait and wait . . .

and wait some more.
How can a minute
take so long?

Frenchy is not as
patient as I am.

So I unwrap one of her presents—
a tug toy.

Frenchy is strong.

But I am stronger.

I pull hard.

Oops!
The tree sways.

Oh no! Oh no!
Look out below!

The tree topper smashes to pieces.
I am devastated, which is upset,
only a zillion times worse.

Just then
Grandpa arrives.
I tell him what
happened.

"When life gives you cracked
eggs, make eggnog," he says.
"What does that mean?" I ask.

"It means you improvise—that's a fancy word for
using whatever's around to make something."

We make a new tree topper with glitter and pom-poms and ribbons.

Grandpa says, "One day you will have your own family, and you will tell them how we made this together."

Oh! "It's going to be an heirloom," I explain to my sister.

Decorating the tree is so much fun. "There's no such thing as too much tinsel!" I keep telling everyone.

Only one word describes how magnificent, joyous, and sparkly Christmas morning is—

splendiferous!